For George Tooker,

whose art made me want to be a painter

Published simultaneously in Canada. Manufactured in China by South China Printing Co. Ltd.

Designed by Gunta Alexander. Text set in Badger Medium.

The art was created with acrylic, oil, and colored pencil on paper.

Library of Congress Cataloging-in-Publication Data

Barron, Rex. Showdown at the food pyramid / written and illustrated by Rex Barron. p. cm.

Summary: When snack foods take over the food pyramid and make it collapse, members of the various food groups have to work together using the Great Food Guide to rebuild it.

[1. Food—Fiction. 2. Nutrition—Fiction.] I. Title. PZ7.B275657Sh 2004 [E]—dc22 2003018321

ISBN 978-0-399-23715-7 10 9 8 7

SHOWDOWN AT THE FOOD PYRAMID

Written and illustrated by

REX BARRON

G. P. Putnam's Sons New York

Once there was a happy and strong food pyramid that worked hard to show people what to eat each day. It was made of all kinds of food, which balanced the pyramid according to the Great Food Guide tacked on the wall.

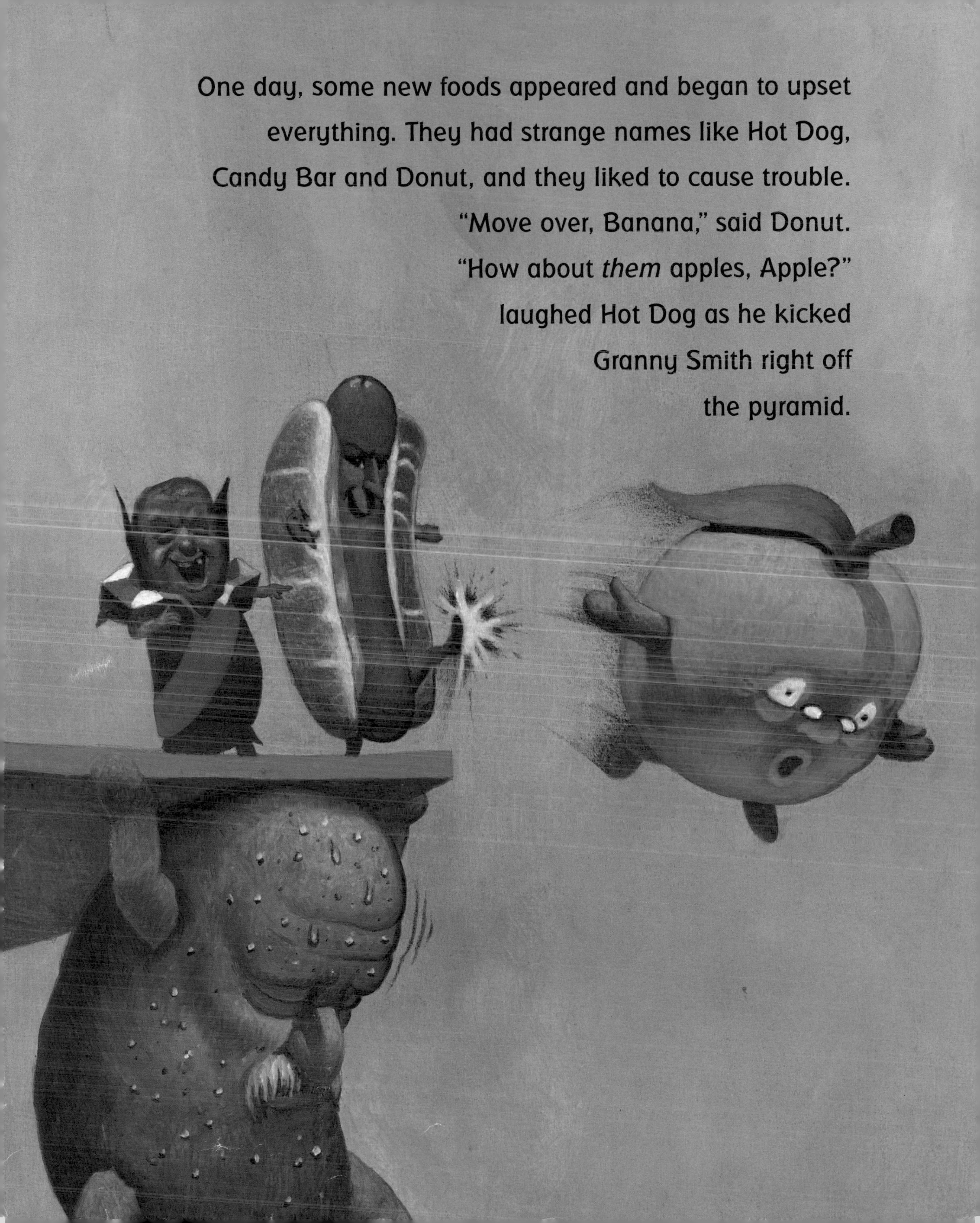

One day, some new foods appeared and began to upset everything. They had strange names like Hot Dog, Candy Bar and Donut, and they liked to cause trouble.

"Move over, Banana," said Donut.

"How about *them* apples, Apple?" laughed Hot Dog as he kicked Granny Smith right off the pyramid.

The big candy bar took over the top floor of the pyramid. "Everybody likes me best," he snickered, "so from now on, I'm *King* Candy Bar. Let's party!"

The fruits and vegetables did not like this at all!

“The pyramid is going to fall over,” said Baby Carrot. “We’ve got to get back on and show King Candy Bar the rules of balance from the Great Food Guide!”

But it wasn't easy. There was just too much food on top.
It looked like the fruits and veggies would
never get back on the pyramid.

Suddenly, there was a loud crash.
The pyramid had collapsed under its own weight!
Donuts and Ice Cream were falling everywhere.
King Candy Bar ended up in the trash!

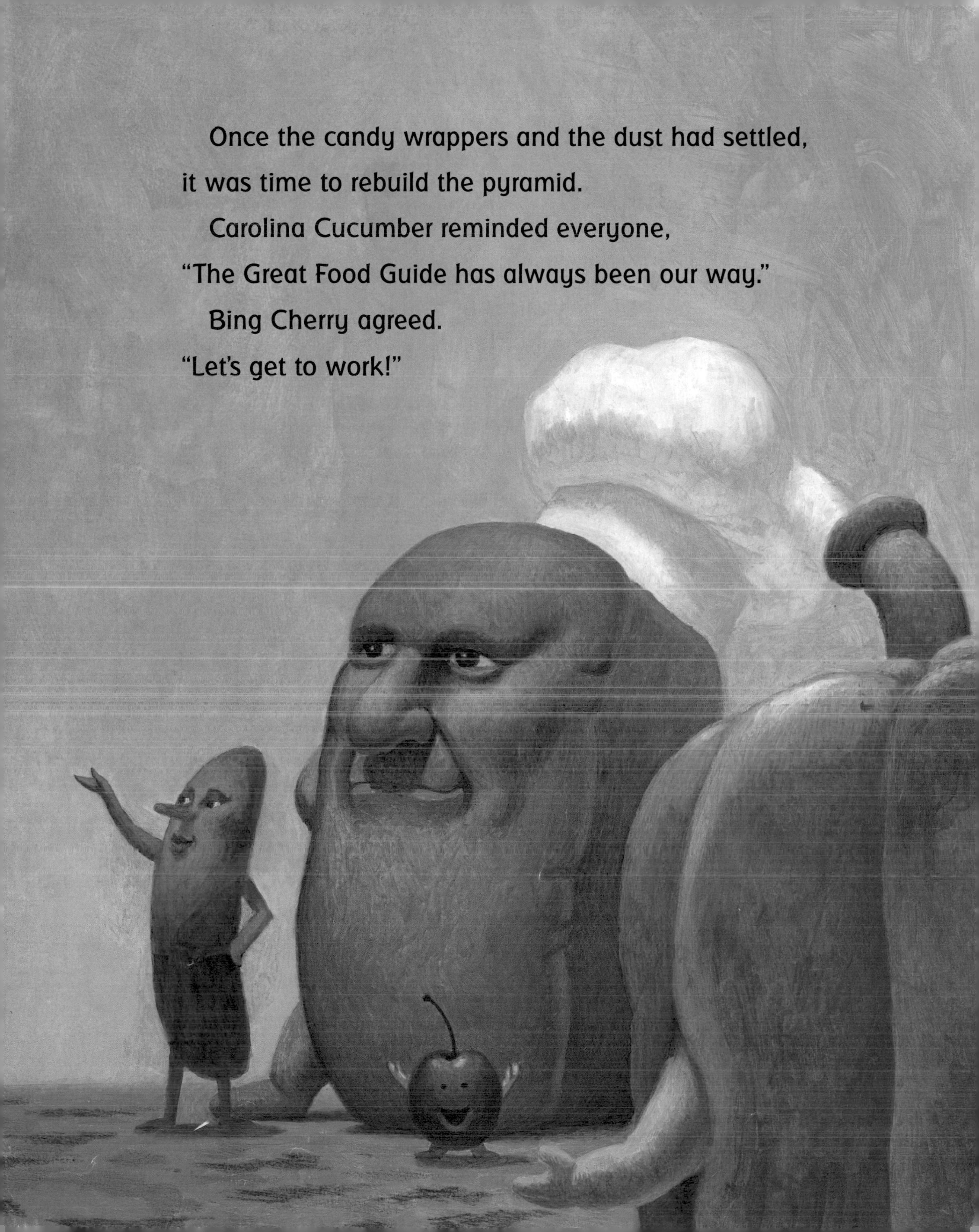

Once the candy wrappers and the dust had settled, it was time to rebuild the pyramid.

Carolina Cucumber reminded everyone, "The Great Food Guide has always been our way."

Bing Cherry agreed. "Let's get to work!"

OATS

The grains were first. Wheat, oats, breads, pasta and rice hold up the other levels and provide lasting energy.

Then came the fruits and vegetables,
brightly colored and full of vitamins.
They fight disease and help
our bodies stay healthy.

YOGU

Finally, the meats and dairy foods took their positions on the third level. Milk, cheeses and yogurt, along with meats and fish, help build kids' muscles and bones. Beans and nuts also belong here. But often they have fat as well as good protein, so less of them are needed.

The pyramid was almost done when
Ice Cream and Cookie came back.
"Please, can we join you?" they asked.
"We're lonely and we miss our old friends."
Some foods were worried.
What if King Candy Bar
followed them back?

In the end, they decided some sweets could return —
but only enough to balance the pyramid on top.
"After all," said Sweet Charlie Strawberry,
"you've got to have *some* variety."

The pyramid was now
strong and happy again.
And when we eat
from this great plan,
we can be strong
and happy, too.

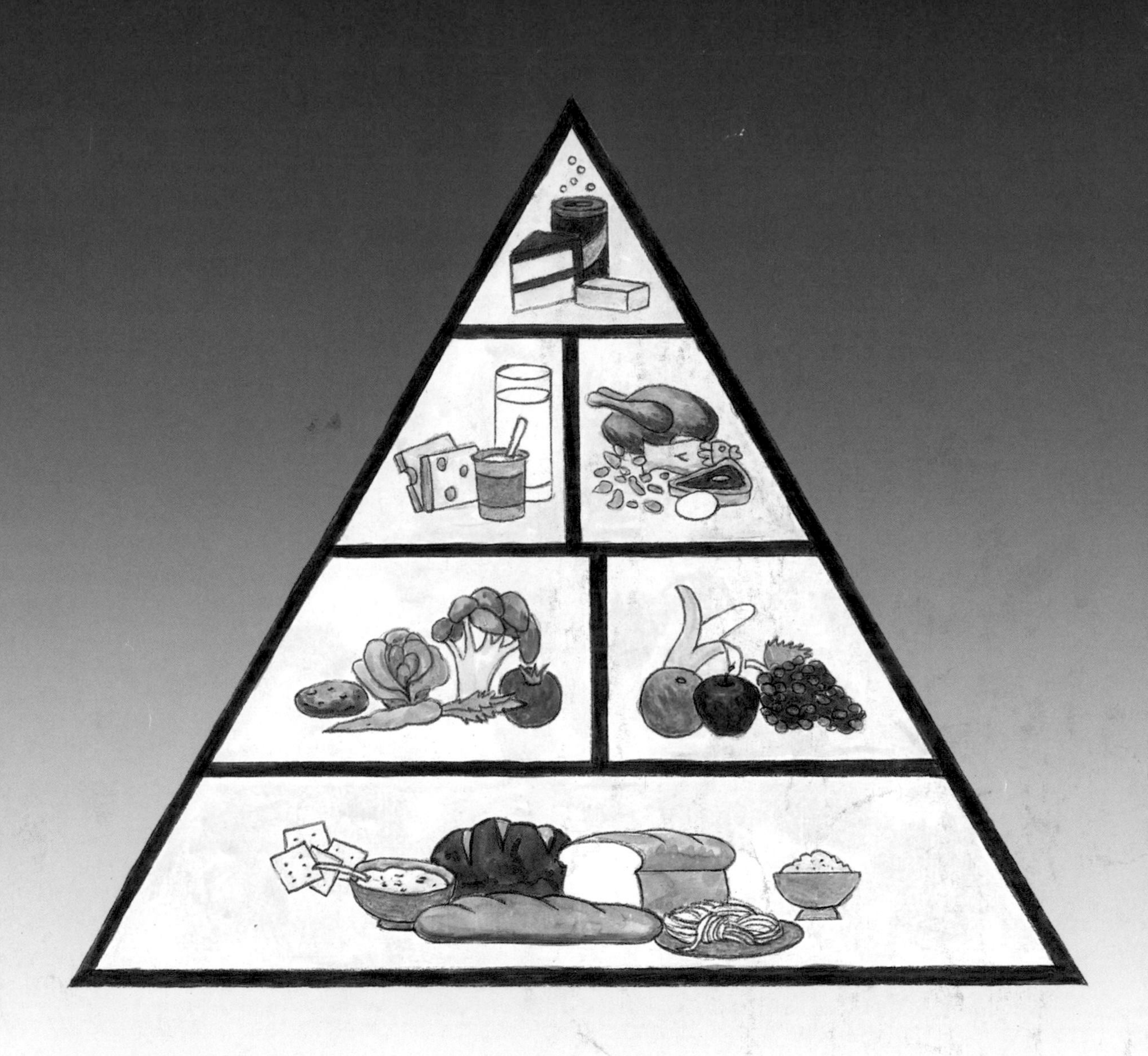

AUTHOR'S NOTE:

This book is based on the Food Guide Pyramid developed by the United States Department of Agriculture as a basic outline of what to eat each day. For more information about the pyramid, nutrition in general, and current recommendations, check out the USDA website at www.usda.gov.